THE KEEPER'S BOOK OF UNUSUAL CREATURES AND OTHER PERTINENT INFORMATION

COMPILED BY BRIDGET BURKE,

DOMINIC AMANDO, WADE CONNELLY,

AND ANNABELLE ELLIS.

KEEPERS OF THE BEASTS

EDITED BY S.G. BOUDREAUX

SCRIBE TO THE NEW EARTH RULERS

S.G. BOUDREAUX

ISBN: 978-1-960091-00-0 (Paperback)

Zanchier Publications

Printed in the USA

Sgboodro2@yahoo.com

www.SGBoudreaux.com

www.Zanchierpublications.com

KEEPER'S NOTE

The Keeper's Book of Unusual Creatures and Other Pertinent Information is an incomplete listing of all the strange creatures we have discovered on our journeys. We Keepers; Bridget Burke, Dominic Amando, Wade Connelly, and Annabelle Ellis; have worked together to bring this manual to existence in hopes that one day, when we are gone and the new Keepers take over, it will be of great assistance to them.

To date, the only odd creatures we have discovered have been those that live mostly in the world of Zanchier. Although we have spent some time on this world, we are certain that there are creatures we have yet to discover and so therefore call this book, as are many of the archives on Reader's Island, an incomplete compilation.

Also contained in this book are images of the covers of the ancient archive books and their keys discovered below Reader's Island in the ancient temple. These books were of the utmost importance in helping us win the Final Battle and have so earned a place in this book. At the end are other images and maps Dominic created for posterities sake. The Bestiary is found just past the archive books.

Now if you are not a Keeper and have managed to get a copy of this book, be forewarned. If you do encounter any of these creatures, they can be deadly so be on your guard; unless of course you are a telepath. Otherwise, you will likely not see these creatures in the wild unless you reside in Zanchier, or you manage to visit the discreetly hidden island of Tanmoyaro Draconomai, which is now where we Keepers reside and care for the Weather Dragons.

Do not attempt time-travel just to glance at these creatures, as it is a deadly business unless you are one of the Chosen. Only the Chosen can walk between worlds by way of storms. And the Portgens have all but been locked away in Simon's New Kingdom Museum to prevent such accidents. Even though Barrier's Edge between worlds has disintegrated since The Chosen won the Final Battle, the world of Zanchier still exists on a fifth-dimension plane and therefore is hard to gain access to. So, I am sorry my friends, but you must simply take our word for the existence of these remarkable creatures.

I, Bridget, did write this book, Dominic sketched and painted the images, Wade observed each creature, figuring out their abilities, and Annabelle compiled all the information from Wade on each beast. This work is our combined efforts. We hope you enjoy learning about these unusual and remarkable creatures.

BOOK OF ARMOR

This book held the prophesy of the Final Battle and explained the search and use for the Armor of God, and the instructions for the Peregrines and Dragoman. It also afforded much needed knowledge and answers to many questions that had plagued the Dragoman for months before the Final Battle. It was the first book to mention the Beast Keepers and to give the Dragoman the knowledge as to what to do with a group of untrainable young people.

BOOK OF ARMOR KEY

THIS KEY IS GOLD AND SILVER.

THE SHAPE OF THE BLADE

IS INSERTED INTO THE IDENTICAL

PLATE AND PUSHED DOWNWARD.

 ONCE YOU HEAR THE

CLICK, THE LOCK SHOULD SPRING

OPEN.

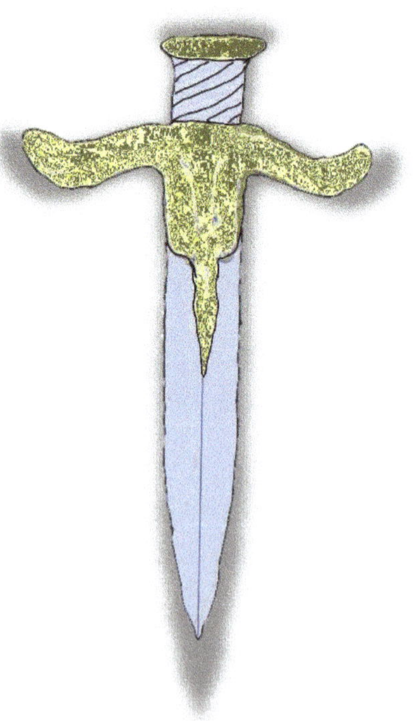

THE KEEPER'S BOOK OF UNUSUAL CREATURES

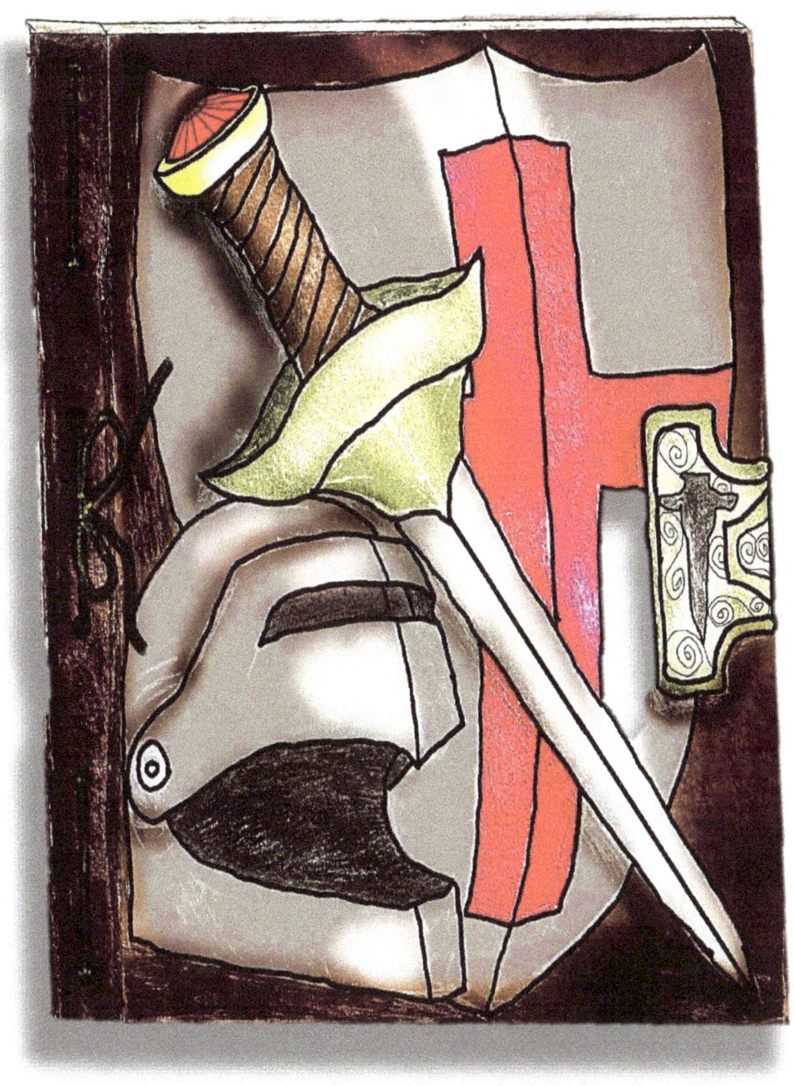

BOOK OF ARMOR

BOOK OF THE KEEPERS

The Beasts Keepers once held the important job as keepers of the Weather Dragons. They were to raise and guide the beasts in love and compassion. The failure of the past Keepers led the Weather Dragons to turn angry, bitter, lonesome, and fearful; throwing the seasons into chaos as storms turned violent and more frequent. The main purpose of the Book of the Keeper's is for instruction to their jobs and where to locate the Weather Dragons.

The Keepers once resided on the island of Tanmoyaro Draconomai in a castle on the eastern cliffs of the coast.
We the Keepers now live there, caring for the Weather Dragon

BOOK OF THE KEEPERS KEY

THE SOLID GOLD KEY IS RECTANGULAR

IN SHAPE AND NEARLY THE SIZE

OF A SMALL GOLD BRICK.

YOU PLACE THE KEY IN THE IDENTICAL

POSITION ON ITS BOTTOM TO THE

MATCHING SYMBOL ON THE BOOK

OF KEEPERS. PUSH DOWN INTO

THE LOCK AND A THIN PIECE OF

METAL RISES AND LOCKS AROUND

THE FIRST LEVEL OF THE KEY,

OPENING THE BOOK.

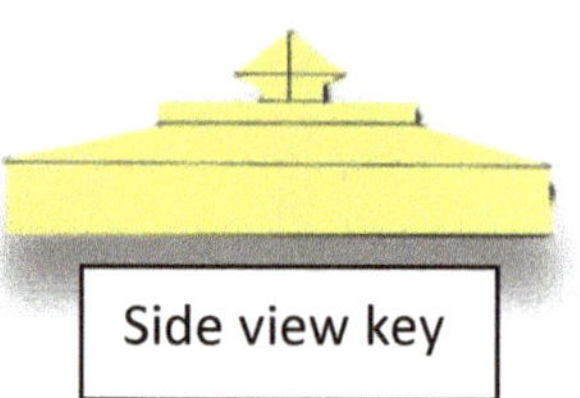
Side view key

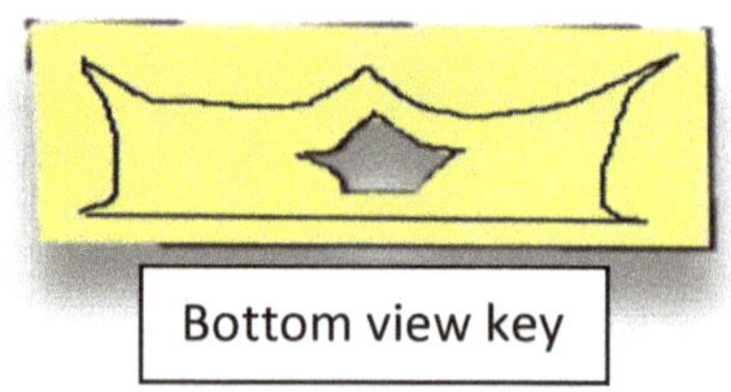
Bottom view key

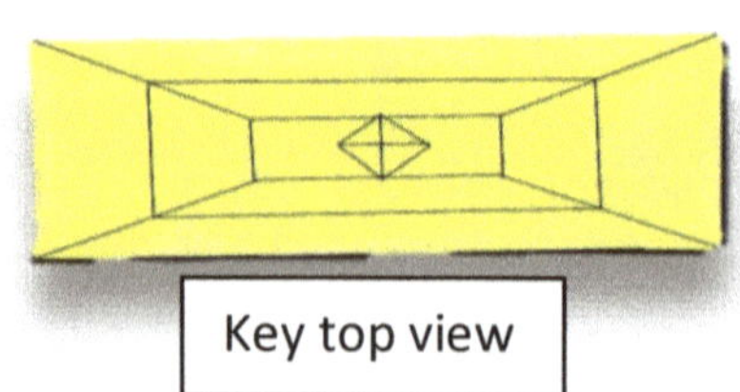
Key top view

BOOK OF THE KEEPERS

BOOK OF LINEAGE

It held intricate, artistic, oil-painted portraits of Peregrines and Dragoman long passed. Simon had never met or heard of the people in this book, but they were no doubt past walkers of the same life we all currently share.

The script in this book looked like the books that monks from the earliest days of transcribing would have created. The first letter of each new biography was beautifully written in a different calligraphy style and finished with gold or silver leafing, or what appeared to be an abrasive, gritty, sand type material. Along the left edge of each page was a beautifully ornate scroll-type border decoration that matched each ornate letter. We know that the first monks who began transcribing books, made them as decorative as possible. They often used gold leaf and crushed or ground gemstones to decorate the lettering and pages. They took great pride and care in their work.

This book held many secret family ties once thought impossible.

BOOK OF LINEAGE KEY

THIS KEY IS MADE OF SILVER AND GOLD.

IT IS ROUND AND MUST BE INSERTED

INTO THE LOCK AND TURNED IN A

SUCCESSION OF MOVEMENTS TO UNLOCK

THE BOOK OF LINEAGE.

THE KEEPER'S BOOK OF UNUSUAL CREATURES

BOOK OF LINEAGE

BOOK OF MYSTERIES

The fourth ancient text was an instruction manual aiding in battle against what appeared to be great beasts. It also mentioned how and where to call upon the "dry bones" mentioned in Ezekial 37:1-10.

This book also gave the Dragoman the knowledge to use some of the more powerful creatures listed in this very book in the great demon battle that took place in Timna Valley, Israel, where many of our beloved and brave Dragoman, Peregrines, and tribal warriors—King Solomon's appointed guards from Memnah's tribe—lost their lives in the last massive demon war.

BOOK OF MYSTERIES KEY

THIS GOLD AND BRASS KEY IS LONG AND THIN. THE SPECIAL PINS AT THE BOTTOM, ONCE INSERTED, ARE SLID SLIGHTLY TO THE RIGHT, UNLOCKING THE TUMBLERS AND THE BOOK.

BOOK OF MYSTERIES

BOOK OF THE BEASTS

The Book of the Beasts was the fifth and final book to be opened by the Dragoman. It gave instructions for the Final Battle. The key had been stolen by a traitor within our tightly knit group of Peregrines and Dragoman, trying to prevent the success of The Twelve in the Final Battle. Once the key was recovered the book lent great instruction to the Dragoman as to what was expected and how to prepare for the fight. This book also holds important information on the Weather Dragons, their role in nature, and their fall from grace and goodness.

BOOK OF THE BEASTS KEY

THIS KEY IS MADE OF BRASS

AND GOLD. TO USE, INSERT THE LIDDED

EYE INTO THE LOCK FACING ON THE

BOOK. WHEN THE EYE IS CLOSED,

THE BOOK IS LOCKED. TURN TO THE RIGHT,

THE MECHANICAL EYE OPENS AND

THE BOOK UNLOCKS.

BOOK OF THE BEASTS

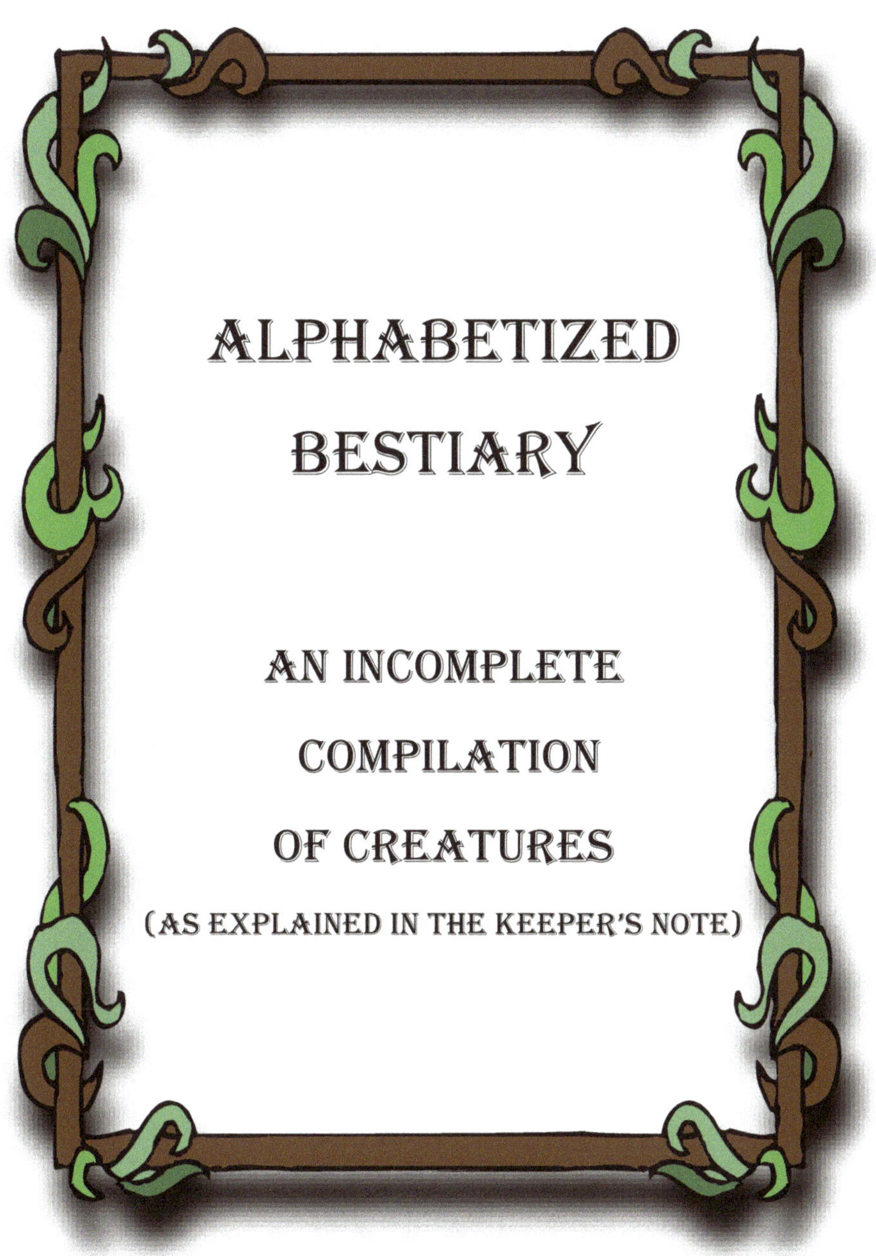

ALPHABETIZED BESTIARY

AN INCOMPLETE COMPILATION OF CREATURES

(AS EXPLAINED IN THE KEEPER'S NOTE)

HARPEE (HAR PY)

Size = Seven feet from claw to ear tip. Wing-span is ten feet.

Coloring = Grayish white, deep blue, or purple

Life span = Ten years.

Main predators = Hungerhounds, Mountain Strikers.

The Harpee is a large predatorial bird, though not quite as large as the Kabihanxu. It lives in the Southern region of the White Mountains of Zanchier. There is little food or vegetation in these mountains making these birds very territorial and likely to attack anyone or anything which wonders near the mountains. No one in Zanchier ever ventures into the White or Bleak Mountains for fear of certain death.

Their feathers are grayish white on their heads and breasts and they have tall, spikey, feather-covered, pointy, ears. They have dark blue or deep purple feathers on their head, neck and wings. Their tallons are long, sharp, and deadly and their beak is pointed and sharp. They use both of these to tear their prey apart.

The Harpee's nest is usually at the top of dead trees since that is nearly all they can find in which to build their nests. They lay one to two eggs a year. They will feed their young for only a few months until they leave the nest to fend for themselves. These birds of prey are soulless creatures with eyes so dark they appear almost hollow, if you can get close enough to see them and survive to tell the tale.

HARPEE

HARPEE CHICK AND EGG

Harpee chicks are born about a month after eggs are laid. Their eggs look like rocks to protect them from would be predators such as the Hungerhound and Mountain Strikers. They are featherless when born but quickly gain their first flight feathers. They must learn to fend for themselves at an early age and if two chicks are born to one nest they will fight one another for the food until only one chick remains. When the chicks fledge and leave the nest, they do not return. They are a lighter blue and white when young and their feathers darken when they become adults.

Survival for a young Harpee can be hard as they have some predators, and food in the White Mountains is scarce. During winter months, the Harpee can have a hard time hiding due to lack of living trees to camouflage themselves, and the striking deep blue or deep purple of the wing feathers stand out against the lighter blue snows of Zanchier. They have no loyalty to any creature and must fight to survive, sometimes even against their own kind.

Native to and found only in Zanchier.

HABITAT AREA WHERE MOSTLY FOUND.

HARPEE CHICK AND EGG

HUNGERHOUND

Size = Seven feet tall from ground to back.

Coloring = Brownish gray fur, grayish white skin.

Life span = Fifteen years.

Main predators = Harpees, and even their own which prey on the weak.

The Hungerhounds are very large, vicious, hunger-driven beasts with hairless heads, and fuzzy, matted, dirty, patches of fur that surround their torsos. Their legs are long and slender with sharp, yellow, claws. Their fanged teeth are sharp and often stained. They live in the Bleak Mountains and hunt the Marshlands and rocky area of Zanchier for whatever food they can find. They usually hunt in packs of five or less and will turn on their own kind if weakness or injury is found. They often will venture into the White Mountains in the southern region in search of other prey.

They can give birth to up to three pups a year. They will train and care for their pups for a year, at which time the pup must either show it's worth to the pack establishing its place in the pecking order or die in the fight becoming the packs next meal.

Legend states that the creatures of Zanchier's southern White and Bleak Mountain regions were once beautiful and friendly, until they were cursed by the evil bestowed upon them by a wicked race of people who once resided in the cities of Miracle and Meribow on the Salt River. These cities were cursed along with the creatures that dwelt near there because of a great evil done long ago. This place now known as the Forgotten Coast and Ruin City is still uninhabitable to this day.

HUNGERHOUND

HUNGERHOUND PUP

Hungerhound pups are born in pairs of two or three. They are born to a vicious lifestyle where they learn to fight early on. Most pups are killed either by their siblings or other pups when learning to fight, or if found to be weak are eaten by the other adult Hungerhounds. Hungerhound packs have very few young who make it to adulthood, keeping the population to a minimum since they are horrid, vicious, beasts. The pups either learn to be mean and tough or they don't survive. They receive very little nurturing care from their parents, making them mean, and angry creatures.

The Hungerhounds dens are beneath and under large rocks and caves in the Bleak Mountains. They cannot swim and fear the water. So much so, they will sacrifice a meal rather than get wet.

They have a sad, heart-wrenching howl that can often be heard piercing the night sky by those who dare travel near the Marshlands or the rocky valley of the Bleak Mountains.

The Gypsies tell the legends of these creatures from many years ago, but only if asked about them.

Native to and found only in Zanchier.

HABITAT AREA WHERE MOSTLY FOUND.

HUNGERHOUND PUP

KABIHANXU (KA BI HAN JU)

Size = Twelve feet in height from claws to head.

Color = Reds, yellows, oranges, purples, and teals,

Life span = Sixty years.

Main Predators = Adult male Pagorinx.

A massive, four-legged, bird-like creature also commonly known as the firebird. It lives in the wilds of Zanchier, mostly around the Xantifal Mountains and the southern regions of the Carpasian Mountains near Treetop Village. They breathe fire and are hard to kill because of their armored skin beneath their colorful plumage. Another power they possess is the ability to harness the power of lightning storms, absorbing the lightning flashes when they feel weak.

These birds of prey have been known to attack fully grown Pagorinxes when food becomes scarce during the winter months. Humans fear them as well, as they can become a food source themselves.

Their beaks are long, sharp, and curved, as are their talons. When in flight, they appear as fire streaking across the sky, their long tail feathers trailing behind them. Adults can also be hunted by man, However many a chick has fallen prey to adult Pagorinxes and other hungry creatures.

They lay two to three eggs every fifth year. They are loving creatures and care for their young until they fledge and leave the nest.

They fly the skies of the mountain ranges in the early mornings and late evenings in search of food. Any who see their shadows on the ground run for cover. Their cries are hauntingly beautiful, sending both awe and fear into the hearts of those that hear it.

KABIHANXU

KABIHANXU CHICK AND EGG

The Kabihanxu chick is a fluffy, colorful, creature. It begins to put on its feathers after just a few days and will fully mature in 6 months. It resembles a colorful ball of fluff until it begins to grow its adult feathers. It will begin to breathe fire when it fledges and leaves the nest. It will stay in the nest until its first flight and will strike out on its own to find a mate. They mate for life, eat meat, and fish, and can grow to an astounding fifteen feet in height, with their tail feathers measuring nearly the length of their bodies.

The Kabihanxu eggs are very colorful in shades of reds, oranges, yellows, purples, and teals. The banded swirls wrap around the egg and the colors blend from one into another. Their surface is relatively smooth with a slight bumpy texture. The eggs are large in size weighing a whopping fifteen pounds.

The Kabihanxu build their nests in the tallest mountain peaks, beneath deep, open, rock ledges far from anything or anyone else.

Some telepathic people, mostly children, have learned to communicate with and ride the creatures of Zanchier.

Native to and found only in Zanchier.

HABITAT AREAS WHERE MOSTLY FOUND.

KABIHANXU CHICK AND EGG

MONSHOKTO (MON SHOCK TOE)

Size = Adult bulls can be up to ten feet tall from the ground to the top of the head when on all fours. When on two legs they are much taller.

Coloring = Browns, tans, and grays.

Lifespan = Thirty years.

Main Predators = Pagorinx, Kabihanxu, and man.

A massive, four-legged creature, that is mainly a land dweller and lives on the edges of Everly Lake, mostly south near Reef Edge Village and further south in the Xantifal Plains. They eat plants and fish and are defensive creatures. They have a near flat face, one horn, and can makes a deep reverberating sound that can repel and immobilize their enemy. Their fur color allows them to appear as boulders on shore. It has a long thick tail, walks upright on two legs, and runs on all four. They can hold their breath for fifteen minutes at a time underwater. Their horn emits an electrical pulse and can also create a protective shield around themselves or their riders. They have webbing beneath the hairy legs on the inside connecting to their torso. They can swim fast and their horn's electrical pulse can surround their rider to create an air bubble underwater.

Although they are defensive, they are not fearful. They will defend their packs and young to the death. They migrate through the Xantifal Mountains across to the other side during the late summer and early fall months in search of certain vegetation that only grows during that time. These herbs are important for the development and growth of the young over the cold, harsh, winter months.

Their horns are often harvested for medicinal purposes. Their meat is used on occasion but only by certain colonies. Their coats are used for clothing and as blankets, usually by the Zanchieth Class.

MONSHOKTO

MONSHOKTO PUP

Monshokto pups are playful creatures who have a natural propensity for exploring and getting into trouble.

They are born with fuzzy hair and a nub for a horn. They grow quickly and will fully mature at six months old. They learn to swim and fish at four weeks old and learn to use their abilities to defend themselves. They will stay with their pod of up to ten Monshokto until they mate and begin their own.

They live in deeply wooded areas, and their dens are located in thick brambles or bushes near boulders and rock facings for safety, but never far from water.

Some get lost while swimming about in Everly Lake for the first time, venturing too far from their mothers; their exuberance for life and adventure lending to many a mishap.

They sleep for long periods of time while they are growing, Eat their weight in vegetation and fish weekly while still nursing on mother's milk.

Their leg webbing, once formed, allows for amazing speed in the water, and they can produce electrical pulses by the time they leave the pod.

You can often hear the pups yowling in the late evenings around Everly Lake practicing their reverberating calls.

Native to and found only in Zanchier.

HABITAT AREAS WHERE MOSTLY FOUND.

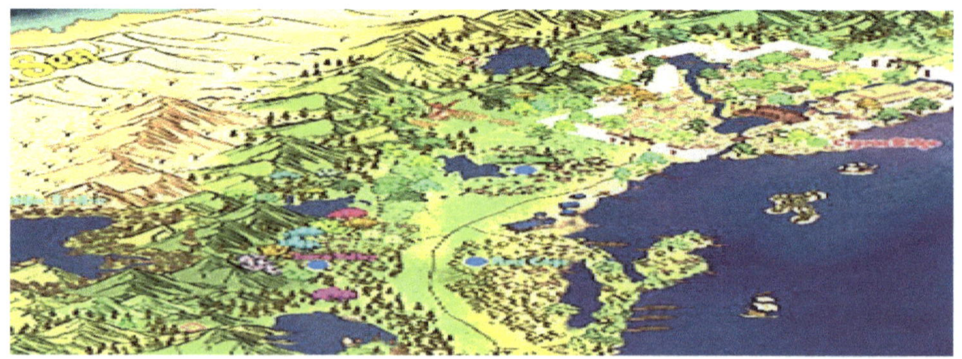

MONSHOKTO PUP

PAGORINX (PA GOR INX)

Size = Eight to ten feet tall from the bottom of the foot to tips of the ears.

Coloring = Black, with white and teal markings.

Life span = Twelve years.

Main predator = Kabihanxu, man, and occasionally a Mountain Striker.

This massive cat-like creature lives in the wilds of Zanchier, mostly around the Xantifal and southern Carpasian Mountains.

They have long sabered teeth on the top row, deep, teal-colored eyes that can mesmerize their prey, long sharp teal, white, and black claws. Their fur is twisted and braided around their head and neck, and they have whitish colored braided looking streaks of fur that run from the tips of their ears to their haunches. They have long tails.

These cats can swim but do not like water. They live near Catamount Gorge in the Xantifal Mountains, and near Treetop Village in the Carpasian Mountains.

Their nests are often in the hollow areas of the large trees, or in the lower, larger, branches. They can have two cubs at a time, but it is rare. They give birth once every two years and Mother and cub lives alone.

Once the cub fully matures, which really depends on the cub, it will leave its mother's care to make its own way. They will however stay in touch as a family unit, until the cub mates and becomes a parent.

Male Pagorinx roam the mountains alone, fighting one another as the dominate male. Only four males exist at a time as the younger ones die in the fight or are picked off as food.

Certain villages will hunt the Pagorinx, using their pelts, meat, and other parts for medicines and other things.

Some telepathic people have learned to communicate and ride the creatures of Zanchier.

PAGORINX

PAGORINX CUB

A Pagorinx cub will stay with its mother until it is fully grown which takes about a year. If it finds a mate, it will leave its mother permanently. It is born as a single cub. It is rare for a Pagorinx to bear twins. Cubs begin to learn to hunt at an early age and will complete their first kill by the age of four months. They can grow to be ten feet tall at the head and weigh three tons; although one this size is rare, and only applies to males.

Pagorinx cubs are born mostly black with only hints of color streaking their fur. The colors and streaks in their fur will appear as they mature.

Pagorinx cubs are playful creatures, tormenting their mothers as they often have no other cubs to play with unless other females in the community have cubs. They will sleep in a pack with each other but hunt and roam the mountains on their own during the day.

No one knows where the Pagorinx community stays as it happens only a few weeks at a time during each season. They mostly roam the mountains, sleeping wherever they find a secure place away from possible Kabihanxu attacks. They will often roam the lower branches of the trees, stalking their prey on the ground below.

They make a purring sound when playing or content. They are fiercely loyal to their own kind and anything that they adopt as their own.

Like many other creatures of Zanchier, their coloring blends in with the many colorful trees that exist in Zanchier, making them hard to see in the upper branches.

NATIVE TO AND FOUND ONLY IN ZANCHIER.

PAGORINX CUB

RAISEDBACK VINDAPER (VIN DU PAIR)

Size = Five feet from the bottom of the foot to the top of the head.

Coloring = Brownish-black,

Life span = No one knows as it is farmed for meat

Main predators = Man, and other larger animals.

A large boar-like animal farmed for its meat, tusks, skins, and medicinal purposes. With three toes on each foot, this six legged animal has three sets of tusks which protrude forward from the back jaw, and upward from the back of the mouth. It is large enough to ride, has brownish-black short hair with a stand of course hair that runs from his head to his tail, decreasing in height near the haunches. It has a long whip-like tail and can be mean tempered. It has little fear of anything in the wild and has been known to take on a Pagorinx. It will fight to the death and is extremely protective of its pups.

The female Vindaper can have an entire litter of pups, up to fifteen at a time. They are separated from their pups as early as possible due to the extreme aggressive nature of the mothers. Farmers have found that if they are separated quickly, then the mothers stay more calm and can be handled and bred more often. But, if a farmer waits too long, the mother will maim or kill the farmer if he or she tries to remove the pups before they mature.

Young Vindaper meat is among the most prized in Zanchier.

The six legs allow the Vindaper to run at amazing speeds for such a heavy stocky creature.

RAISEDBACK VINDAPER

RAISEDBACK VINDAPER PUPS

Vindaper pups are born in clusters of six to fifteen at a time. Most Vindapers are born to farm raised animals. Few are found in the wild unless they escape their captivity and survive the wilds of Zanchier.

Pups are precocious creatures, They are playful, rambunctious, and seem to find trouble around every turn. They learn to fight at a young age, usually tormenting one another to establish the pecking order.

As they grow into juveniles, they become more aggressive toward the other pups in the pack. In farming communities it is the pups that have reached near full maturity that are farmed for meat. Some of the best animals are kept for continued breeding, and the parents retired, usually to live out the remainder of their lives in pasturelands.

Native to and found only in Zanchier.

RAISEDBACK VINDAPER PUP

TARPHAMOOR (TAR FA MORE)

Size = Six feet from hoof to horn.

Coloring = Deep gray with bright purple and red stripes.

Life span = Eight years.

Main predator = Man, and other large creatures.

The Tarphamoor is a ram-like creature hunted for its beautiful, colorful pelts. The have one long curving horn that sits in the center of the head but curves to one side at the top and then turns to the other as it grows, balancing out the weight of it.

Its unique horn is used as a type of trumpet, and their sweet, white meat is often considered a delicacy . Their organs and other parts are also used for medicinal purposes.

The average height of a Tarphamoor is five foot high at the top of the neck. But some bulls can reach six feet.

They are offensive creatures and very territorial. Not many people farm them due to their combative nature. Males will fight all day long for position of lead Tarphamoor, often doing damage to each other, reducing the price of the horns.

Farmers who do attempt to raise them must keep them separated from each other to get the best price for unmarked horns and pelts.

Some Tarphamoor do roam wild and walk the open plains of Zanchier grazing on grasses and other vegetation. They bed down under large trees out in the open. Their stubbornness and combative attitudes usually cost them their lives and the lives of their young from predators.

They can have up to three kids at a time and often do. A single kid is a rare sight.

TARPHAMOOR

TARPHAMOOR KID

Tarphamoor kids are exact replicas of their parents, except that their horns take a few months to form. They use their nubs to butt heads with other kids and any stationary object.

As adults, they use their horns as defense and to fight for position of lead Tarphamoor. They eat grass and other vegetation.

Kids spend their days romping and playing in the fields and lower mountain areas, often finding themselves in trouble on a weekly basis.

Many juveniles have been known to try to take on fully grown mountain strikers. Few have succeeded.

Farmers try to keep the kids in pens with taller walls as they are masters at escaping.

The meat of juvenile Tarphamoors can taste gamey until they reach a certain age.

The colorful pelts are prized by the Bakrisian dignitaries from the city of Cypress Ridge.

Native to and found only in Zanchier.

HABITAT AREA WHERE MOSTLY FOUND.

TARPHAMOOR KID

TREFELL (TRE FELL)

Size = Two feet in every direction.

Coloring = Brown (varies).

Life span = Twelve years.

Predators = Any and all meat eaters.

A Beaver-like, medium sized, extremely furry animal that looks like a ball of fuzz rolling around on the ground. It has a protruding pinkish-white nose, and long, sharp, curved teeth. It is so furry you can barely see the creature's eyes.

They dwell near the rivers and uninhabited areas of Everly Lake, Catamount Gorge, and any and all other waterfalls or water sources throughout Zanchier.

They are hunted for their pelts, meat, and for other medicinal qualities.

They can have up to six young at a time, although it is rare to have more than four. They mate for life with one partner and live together as a family unit until each pup finds its own mate and begins to build its own nest.

They can chew through small trees within thirty minutes and build their nest in a single day. They eat fruits, nuts, berries, fish, and other green leafy plants.

They are docile creatures who will hide when startled. They are in no way aggressive and won't normally bite unless cornered and frightened.

When they want to move great distances quickly, they roll into a ball and roll along the ground at great speeds. They can work their back muscles and thick fur like a steering mechanism and an occasional leg or foot in the right direction helps as well.

They have a built-in navigational system that aids them in the correct direction when in rolling mode. They also float on top of the water for several minutes in rolling mode as well, their poofy fur acting like a natural barrier. When unfurled, they can sink or dive deep very quickly.

TREFELL

TREFELL PUP

Trefell pups are born hairless with no teeth. They begin to grow hair and teeth after one week. By four weeks of age they are beginning to gnaw on any wood they find. They mature at five months old and will stay with the family unit until they find a mate.

Trefell pups are adventurous at first until taught to be evasive.

They are usually scared of sudden noises, intruders, and open bright areas.

They tend to stick to heavily wooded areas and waterways due to being small and easy pickings for other predators.

Pups are fat little furry creatures, but until their fur fully grows their legs and eyes are clearly visible. They can tuck into a ball to protect their more sensitive and vulnerable parts against predators and their thick fur can actually protect against sharp teeth and claws.

Native and found only in Zanchier.

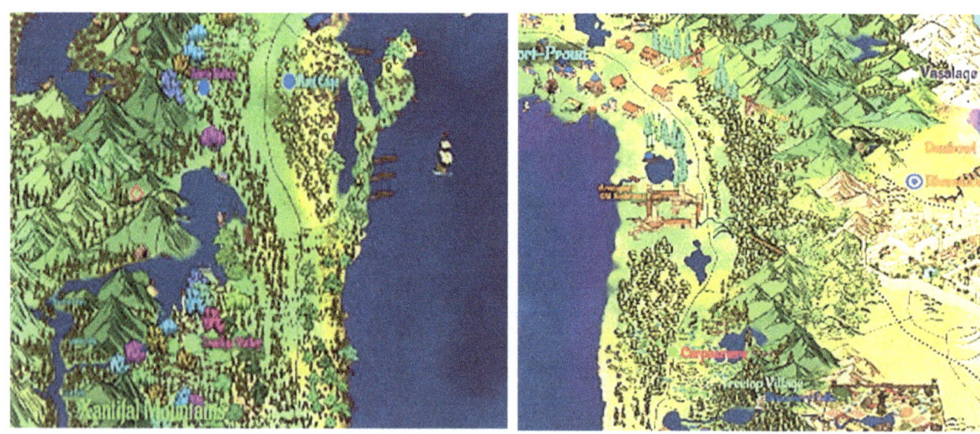

TREFELL PUP

TRIBHON (TRI BUN)

Size = They average two feet tall and four feet in length including the tail,

Coloring = Brownish-gray fur with reddish-orange stripes.

Life span = Twenty years.

Predators =Many omnivores.

A small to medium sized animal, bigger than a squirrel but smaller than a raccoon. It has a long, hairy, skinny tail that it can use to hold onto things. This tail also has a retractable stinger, which it uses to temporarily paralyze its victims. It has long, sharp, retractable claws, opposable thumbs on the front claws, and are light in weight. They can move fairly quickly on both ground and in trees. It lives in the forest of the surrounding mountain ranges and can camouflage to its surroundings.

A Tribhon usually mates for life and has one or two pups at a time.

They make their nests in the middle branches of certain trees, usually finding hollowed out areas, splits, or abandoned nests.

They are scavengers, eating mostly shellfish, fish, and vegetation. Their favorite meal is Riverbrine.

They can be playful, but easily get bored and turn spiteful.

They live in small communities of about fifteen for safety purposes.

TRIBHON

TRIBHON PUP

Tribhon pups are born with some fur but are light in color.

They have short opposable thumbs on their front paws only and can cling onto branches and other objects. They can also climb most objects relatively well with their sharp claws.

Tribhon pups begin defensive learning when they are only three weeks old. They grow their long claws and poison spike by the age of four weeks. A Tribhon can grow to a height of three feet, not including the lengths of their equally long tales.

They eat vegetation, fish, and other shellfish. They are defensive creatures but will attack if threatened.

They will continue to live in their parents community until such a time as they are old enough to leave. Some may find mates within their parental community, but often will join their mates community instead.

As older Tribhon die off or get killed, the younger ones will fight for the leadership position of the community.

Native to and found only in Zanchier.

HABITAT AREA WHERE MOSTLY FOUND.

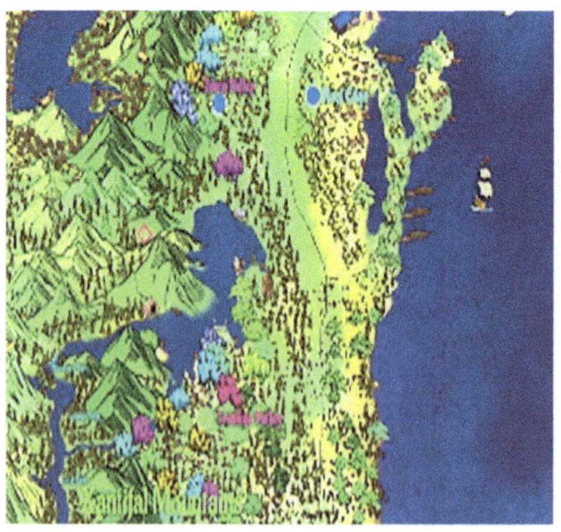

TRIBHON PUP

YAREQUU (YAR A KOO)

Size = Large, rideable beast. Stands twenty to twenty-five hands high.

Coloring = Grayish with hints of teal in the neck, face, ears, and mane and tail.

Life span = Twenty years.

Main predators = Kabihanxu and Pagorinx.

The Yarequu resembles a horse but is much larger. The average Yarequu stands twenty to twenty-five hands high and has a width of up to eight hands. It is larger than a Clydesdale, has three-toed split hooves, braided, twisted mane and tail, and has spikes that slant upward at each leg at the knee joint. It is charcoal in color with streaks of white and teal around its eyes, ears, and mouth, and running down its neck, fanning out and blending into its coat. These streaks are also evident around its hooves and the spikes on its legs. When threatened it has a camouflaging ability for itself and its riders. The spikes on its legs open into a small, strong, shield that allows the Yarequu to glide through the air if up high. They do not flap or fly.

Yarequu are mainly bred on farms in Zanchier, the largest of which exists on the western edge of Everly Lake just above Cypress Ridge Village. Some Yarequu do roam wild in Zanchier, mostly around the open plains at the base of the Xantifal Mountains. Yarequu are pack animals and used to pull carts and help to plow fields for the lower classed citizens of Zanchier.

YAREQUU

YAREQUU FOAL

Yarequu foals are spirited young creatures. When they are born they learn to stand quickly to flee from danger. Their coats are a dull grayish black at first, then as they get older they begin to get their coloring of light gray and teal blue. Some Yarequu foals coloring can differentiate by depth of hue and color but are usually consistent. By two months old they are trained to use the gliders that open at the knee joint. Most foals are brave as they are spirited creatures, but some have been known to need a push from the mountain ledge to get them to learn to use their gliders. They also can be mischievous, using their camouflage abilities to hide from their parents.

Native to and found only in Zanchier.

YAREQUU FOAL

ZIPPLEWHIP

Size = Eight foot in height.

Coloring = Deep purple, blue, and red, but colors can vary with shades of yellow and gold, and shades of varying greens.

Life span = Five years on average largely due to lack of intelligence.

Main Predators = Man, and other larger beasts.

A large flightless bird which uses its bulbus, hard, head to punch and hit. It gets its name from the sound its head makes when it whips around to hit you. A loud zipping, rattling, sound preludes a hard smack from the bird, sending its adversaries sailing. They make a decent meal but the breast meat is the only thing palatable as their legs and head are mostly bone. Their feathers are often sold in markets as decorations or for rainproofing coats. As they dip their long gangly necks to fish, they may have to swim a little bit when necessary but never stray too far from the shore, Side flaps in the long skinny neck open underwater, wrapping around larger schools of fish like a net.

Both parents will sit on the eggs and tend to the chicks so distinguishing the males from the females is something we have not been able to determine as of yet. More research must be done on these strange birds.

Their eggs are usually harvested to make omelets and the like. Their eggs are large enough to feed several people, since one egg is twice as large as a football.

They are normally non-combative unless provoked or feel they need to protect their young, which is a constant chore.

They can run extremely fast at approximately fifty miles an hour, making them nearly impossible to catch. However, they are not very intelligent, making them an easy hunting target.

ZIPPLEWHIP

ZIPPLEWHIP CHICK AND EGG

Zipplewhip chicks are normally born in large clutches of ten to fifteen eggs to a single set of parents. They are born a light pink, yellow, or green color and when they get older their feathers will darken to a deep purple, gold, or forest green, and the headnub and legs will darken as well. Some nubs can be very colorful while others can be a drab gray color or black. We have not determined yet whether this differentiating color has to do with the male or female population as of yet since it is hard to determine which is which.

Chicks will play with their hard nubbed heads, butting one another or other inanimate objects until they pass out. This is usually a good thing for the adult birds as it gives them a break from the constant gathering and herding of the chicks.

In the spring, Zipplewhips migrate and gather together for colonization, at which time all the chicks hatch, which makes it difficult for the parents to keep their own clutches together. Many times, chicks can get mixed up between all the adults and they will end up raising each other's chicks. This situation does not cause any harm or issues as many colonies stay together until the chicks are old enough to fend for themselves. Then the adults will separate and the now juvenile chicks will pair up with a mate and venture out into the wilds of Zanchier until the following spring.

Many juvenile chicks will not survive on their own, as said before, they are not intelligent birds. They fall prey to many wild animals and are usually hunted for food by many of the people of Zanchier. A Few people even farm the birds with some difficulty as the birds usually destroy any shelter they are given by the continual activity of the nub butting chicks, and the occasional show of haughtiness by the adults as well.

Eggs have colorful bands in shades of purple and teal that wrap around the surface in a circular pattern.

Native to and found only in Zanchier.

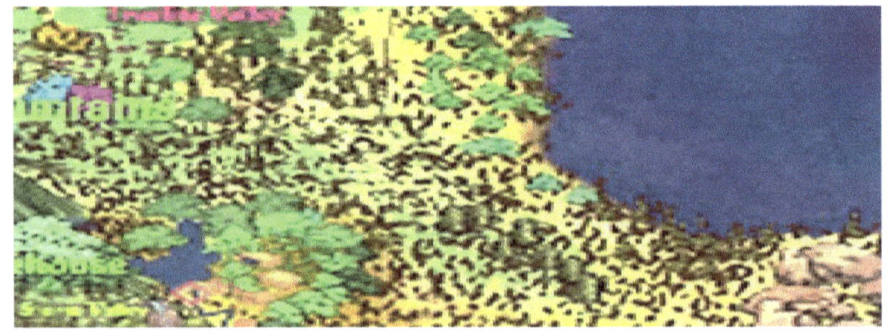

ZIPPLEWHIP CHICK AND EGG

EARTH DRAGON

Size = Largest creature to ever roam the earth.

Coloring = Earthen brown, and mossy green.

Life span = Eternal until it chooses to die and pass the torch to the next one to be born.

Main Predators = None.

The Earth dragon is the beast that controls earthquakes and sinkholes throughout the earth. It was once a beautiful creature when its Keeper was attentive and selfless. Special humans known as Keepers were meant to be their caregivers and companions, but once long ago, their Keepers turned their backs on the weather dragons and they all turned dark and evil. As man's sin grew, so did the agitation of the beasts.

The Earth Dragon is a flightless beast with four eyes that can see in a three-hundred-and-sixty-degree radius. It lives on the surface of Tanmoyaro Draconomai and builds its nest on the ground in the dense forest which surrounds the high mountain.

It is the largest of all four weather dragons, so massive that one of the Peregrines rode a Yarequu up its tale to its back to do battle, during which, one of the Dragon's protruding teeth flew from its mouth in the battle, and stuck into the ground next to a Keeper. The broken tooth was larger than the young man.

Native to and found only on Tanmoyaro Draconomai.

EARTH DRAGON

EARTH DRAGON HATCHLING AND EGG

Weather dragons lay only one egg at a time, and the egg will not hatch until the adult dragon has passed. It then will hatch to take the place of the deceased dragon as the new ruler of the weather.

The earth dragon hatchling will progress quickly in size over a few months' time. It reaches its adult size of a two-story building within six months. However, as they live long lives, they will continue to grow slowly over the course of their lifespan. They are vegetarians and eat mostly plant life but will eat fish on occasion.

Native to and found only on Tanmoyaro Draconomai.

EARTH DRAGON HATCHLING AND EGG

FIRE DRAGON

Size = Immeasurable as they grow continually but slowly over their lifespan.

Coloring = Red and orange.

Life span = Eternal until it chooses to die and pass the torch to the next one to be born.

Main Predators = None.

The Fire Dragon is the beast that controls the volcanoes throughout the earth. It was once a beautiful creature when its Keeper was attentive and selfless. Special humans known as Keepers were meant to be their caregivers and companions, but once the Keepers turned their backs on the weather dragons, they all turned dark and evil. As man's sin grew, so did the agitation of the beasts.

The Fire Dragon has been trapped beneath the earth's surface, alone in a cave for hundreds of years. Her wings are tattered and torn from lack of use and neglect. Her scales are thick and nearly impenetrable and much of her face and tale is covered in spikes. She is angry, lonely, and miserable, and yearns for revenge.

Native to and found only on Tanmoyaro Draconomai.

FIRE DRAGON

FIRE DRAGON HATCHLING AND EGG

Weather dragons lay only one egg at a time, and the egg will not hatch until the adult dragon has passed. It then will hatch to take the place of the deceased dragon as the new ruler of the weather.

The Fire Dragon's nest is in a deep cave at the base of the Tanmoyaro Mountains. The hatchling will emerge from the dark cavern, making the long journey up and out of the mountain in search of food. It will continue to slowly grow until its death. The fire dragon prefers hot weather.

The interior of the broken egg looks like a geode inside.

Native to and found only on Tanmoyaro Draconomai.

FIRE DRAGON HATCHLING AND EGG

WATER DRAGON

Size = Immeasurable as they grow continually but slowly over their lifespan.

Coloring = Red, blue, brown, and black.

Life span = Eternal until it chooses to die and pass the torch to the next one to be born.

Main Predators = None.

The water dragon, or Leviathan, is the beast that controls the tsunamis, hurricanes, and waterspouts throughout the earth. It was once a beautiful creature when its Keeper was attentive and selfless. Once the Keepers turned their backs on the weather dragons they all turned dark and evil. As man's sin grew, so did the agitation of the beasts.

The water dragon is a flightless beast that, for some reason, has been more disfigured than the other three dragons. It's successor looks nothing like the adult that was fought and overcome in the Final Battle.

This beast has the torso and legs of a crab, the forearms of an octopus, and a triangular shaped head with horns and jaw spikes covered in barnacles. Its sharp teeth protrude from its mouth in all directions.

It has blue spiked ridges that run from the shoulders to the tail, which is split into three parts on the end, and has round balls covered in spikes which it uses to pound the ocean floor to create tsunamis, and earthquakes.

Native to and found only on Tanmoyaro Draconomai.

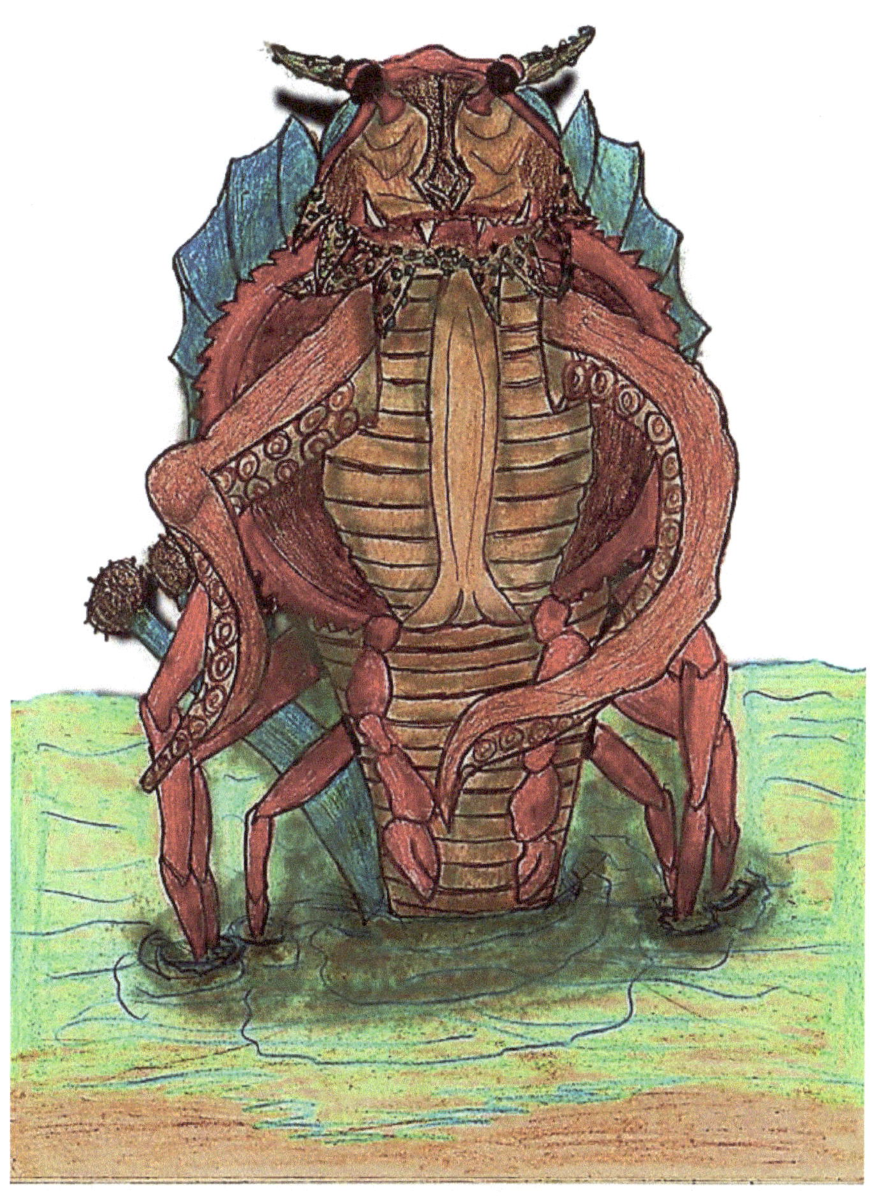

WATER DRAGON

WATER DRAGON HATCHLING AND EGG

Weather dragons lay only one egg at a time, and the egg will not hatch until the adult dragon has passed. It then will hatch to take the place of the deceased dragon as the new ruler of the weather.

The nest is laid in an underwater cavern amongst seaweed and rock. Hatchlings are a beautiful sea blue in color and have a smooth, dolphin-like skin. They have a three way split tail with smooth hard balls on the tips they use to pound the sea floor and stir the waters to create tidal waves and storms. They can breathe both air and water, but their skin will dry out if left out of water too long.

Native to and found only on Tanmoyaro Draconomai.

WATER DRAGON HATCHLING AND EGG

WIND DRAGON

Size = Immeasurable as they grow continually but slowly over their lifespan.

Coloring =White with soft shades of blue.

Life span = Eternal until it chooses to die and pass the torch to the next one to be born.

Main Predators = None.

The Wind Dragon is the beast that controls tornadoes, ice storms, and sandstorms throughout the earth. It was once a beautiful creature when its Keeper was attentive and selfless. Once the Keepers turned their backs on the weather dragons they all turned dark and evil. As man's sin grew, so did the agitation of the beasts.

The Wind Dragon lives at the top of the floating mountains of Tanmoyaro Draconomai. It spits ice and throws ice spikes with its tail. It is the smallest of all four weather dragons, and being white, it can camouflage amongst the clouds. Its teeth and claws are black and sharp. It has three ridges that run from the nose to its shoulders.

It's powerful wings circulate the winds and creates storms throughout the earth's realms and dimensions.

Native to and found only on Tanmoyaro Draconomai.

WIND DRAGON

WIND DRAGON HATCHLING AND EGG

Weather dragons lay only one egg at a time, and the egg will not hatch until the adult dragon has passed. It then will hatch to take the place of the deceased dragon as the new ruler of the weather.

The wind dragon hatchling will eat whatever it can scrounge in the floating mountains until it learns to fly. It will then fly to the mountain's base and hunt for small creatures and fish then returns to its cave at the top of the mountain, As the youngling matures, its bluish coloring slowly fades to white the older it gets.

Native to and found only on Tanmoyaro Draconomai.

WIND DRAGON HATCHLING AND EGG

GRASS STRIKER AND EGGS

The grass striker is a green snake that is non-poisonous. It attacks and kills other poisonous snakes. It makes its nest in holes in the ground or in the hollowed-out undersides of living trees or fallen timber. It lays a total of up to ten eggs with each nest it makes. It will pack its nest with small dead animals for its young to feed on when they hatch. The eggs are grayish brown with small green spots that give them a mossy rock appearance which deters predators.

Native to and found only in Zanchier.

HABITAT AREAS WHERE MOSTLY FOUND.

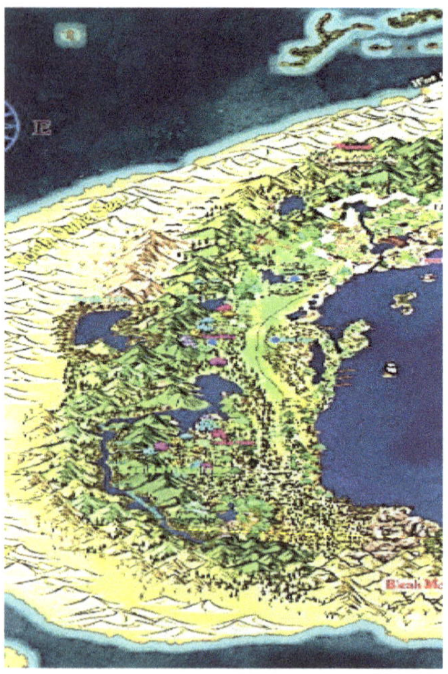 

GRASS STRIKER AND EGGS

MOUNTAIN STRIKER AND EGGS

Mountain strikers are grayish in color and are most poisonous when young. An adult mountain striker can reach fifteen feet long and has a thick body. It moves more slowly the larger it becomes. They have been known to grow large enough to take down the pups and kids of the Monshokto and Tarphamoors. Their eggs are gray and appear to be rocks, which often protect them from predators.

Native to and found only in Zanchier.

HABITAT AREAS WHERE MOSTLY FOUND.

MOUNTAIN STRIKER AND EGGS

SAND STRIKER AND EGGS

Sand Strikers move sideways quickly in a rolling pattern and will chase after anything no matter the size. Most other animals tend to avoid them as they are very aggressive creatures, Their bites are poisonous with some being fatal depending on the size of its victim. Their nests are buried beneath the sand in cooler shady spots. They have triangular shaped scales and a bumpy or spikey appearance. Their eggs are relatively flat and are a creamy gray color with yellow dots in the middle which gives them the appearance of a cracked hen egg.

Native to and found only in Zanchier.

HABITAT AREAS WHERE MOSTLY FOUND.

SAND STRIKER AND EGGS

TREE STRIKER AND EGGS

Tree Strikers are non-poisonous, grow long, and have a flat appearance. They can maneuver tree branches very well due to their flat-like bodies. They feed on rodents, birds, and other smaller animals. They are able to camouflage to their surroundings. Their nests are built in the forest in heavily wooded areas in any type of wood structure. They lay around ten eggs per cycle and they cycle five times a year. Their eggs are brown with yellow spots.

Native to and found only in Zanchier.

HABITAT AREA WHERE MOSTLY FOUND.

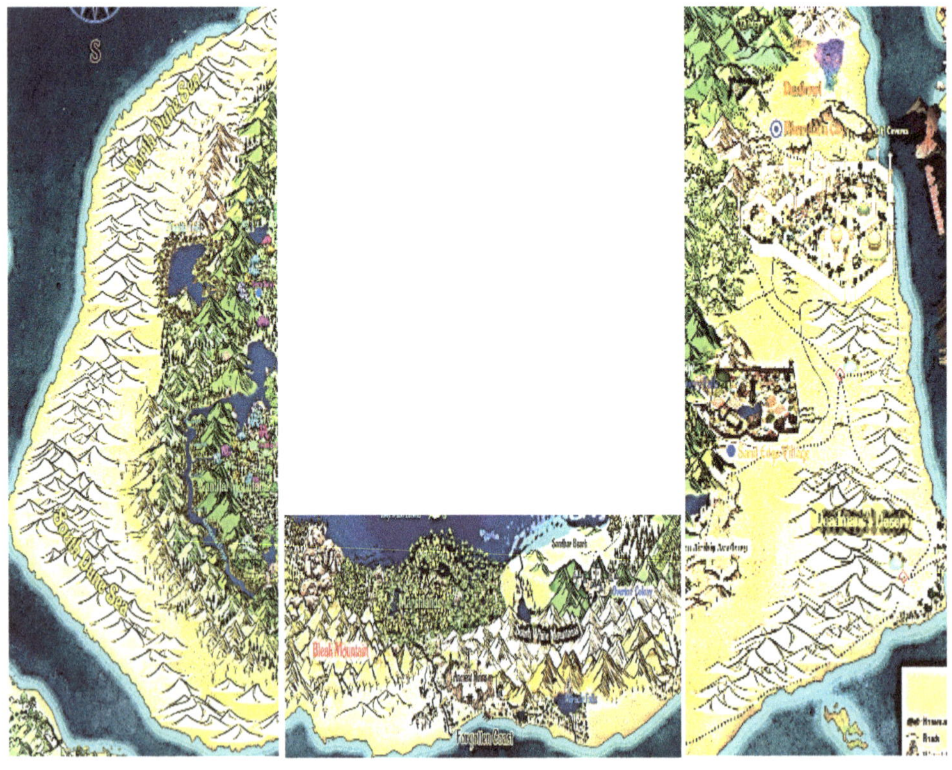

TREE STRIKER AND EGGS

WATER STRIKER AND EGGS

Water strikers are found more frequently in the Marshlands and less frequented areas of Zanchier. They are very poisonous and their victims can die quickly depending on their size. A fully grown man, who fails to find treatment for a bite within five hours, may perish. They lay their eggs in thick grassy areas of the marsh and around mangrove plant roots. They lay up to fifty eggs at a time, but many get eaten by fish before they hatch. The eggs are a glossy, iridescent blue and appear more translucent when close to hatching.

Native to and found only in Zanchier.

HABITAT AREA WHERE MOSTLY FOUND.

WATER STRIKER AND EGGS

BIO-JUMPER

Jumpers are froglike creatures with many different varieties and appearances that reside all over Zanchier.

The Bio-Jumper, specifically, lives in the bioluminescent world beneath the Marshlands on the southern border of Everly Lake. They can jump long distances in a single bound because of the webbing on the underside of their body attached to their legs, making them appear to fly. This webbing also works like underwater wings which allow them to move quickly in the water.

These bioluminescent creatures have not been studied much due to the lack of ability to reach the world beneath the Marshlands of Zanchier. Most of our records concerning these creatures were found in books that were located in an old facility once known as the Loradin Animal Rescue and Sanctuary, or LARS for short. These books were purchased on one of our trips to Zanchier from some wandering gypsies that roam the land.

Native to and found only in Zanchier.

HABITAT AREA WHERE MOSTLY FOUND.

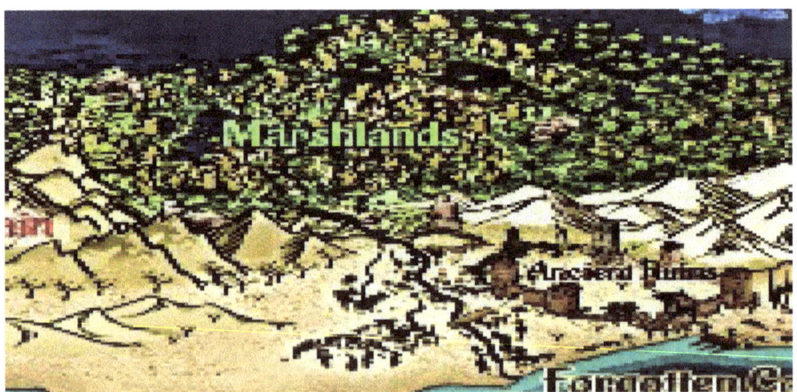

BIOLUMINESCENT JUMPER

BIO-STRIKER

Bio-Strikers live in the bioluminescent world beneath the Marshlands of Zanchier on the southern border of Everly Lake. Most tree varieties are harmless and eat small animals. They spend their lives sleeping during the daylight hours, hanging from trees by the ends of their tails or by wrapping their bodies around a branch. They dangle from branches like vines, camouflaging themselves to their surroundings.

Native to and found only in Zanchier.

HABITAT AREA WHERE MOSTLY FOUND.

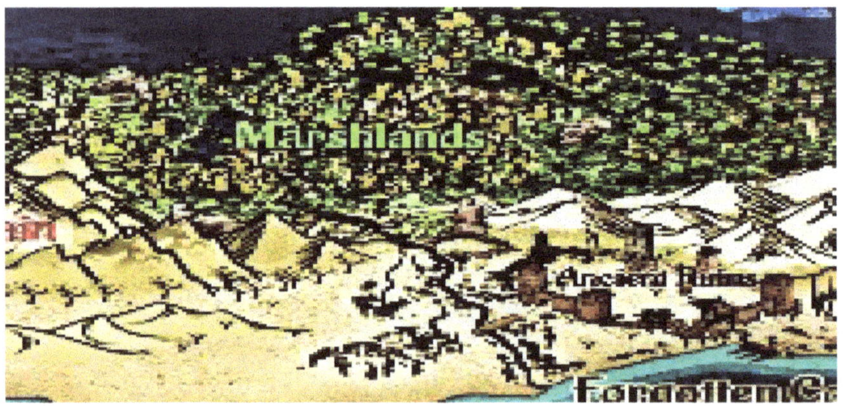

BIOLUMINESCENT STRIKER

SPIRITFLY

The Spiritfly resembles a butterfly, except that it flutters much more slowly through the air with its long, flowing wings, giving it the appearance of floating underwater.

It is approximately twelve to fifteen inches in length. It only lives beneath the Marshlands in a bioluminescent, air-filled, cavern known to very few humans. This bioluminescent world is also home to the Brindelwren and many other bioluminescent creatures and plant life.

Their colors and shapes are varied.

Native to and found only in Zanchier.

HABITAT AREA WHERE MOSTLY FOUND.

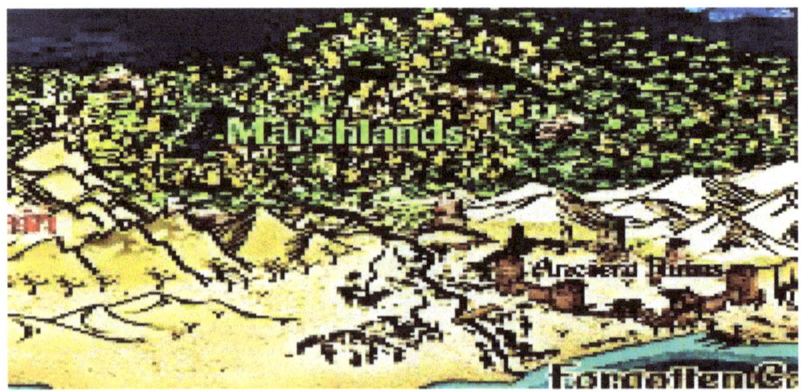

BIOLUMINESCENT SPIRITFLY

BRINDELWREN

Size = Forty feet in length, twenty feet in height from belly to head.

Coloring = Green and brown.

Life Span = Unknown.

Main Predators = None.

The largest of all Zanchier's creatures, the Brindelwren lives in Everly Lake, which sits in the center of Zanchier.

The Brindelwren is rarely seen unless it wants to be. The kelpy strands on its head and around its fins flow like hair. Its head resembles that of a seahorse, and its long body is like that of an eel. It can vanish quickly with its cloaking abilities. It has long, sinewy, flowing fins, and a long, poisonous tail that can produce spikes from beneath the kelpy strands. It is bioluminescent when it wants to be. It has been known to sink ships, and sailors refer to it as the Sea Beast.

The Bridelwren swims in underwater caverns beneath the Marshlands that leads to the oceans which surround the world of Zanchier. This is why it is rarely seen; that and its cloaking ability of course. It is believed to be the last of its kind. It lives in the bioluminescent world that exists below the dreaded Marshlands. This bioluminescent world gives the Marshlands an eerie orangish glow at night, which is one of the things which keep people away and causes them to call it cursed.

Some telepathic people have learned to communicate and ride the creatures of Zanchier.

Native to and found only in Zanchier and surrounding oceans.

BRINDELWREN

GLOWFISH

Size = Approximately twenty-four to thirty inches in length.

Coloring = Green and greenish blue.

Life Span =Varies.

Main Predators = Man, and larger fish.

Glowfish are bioluminescent fish that mainly live in the streams and tributaries of Luminesce Falls; but now invade Everly Lake. These stinging fish with five long tentacled arms are attracted to sparkly items; anything that glimmers in the sunlight. They wrap their tentacles around their pray and infuse them with poison which swells and reddens the skin, killing their prey within minutes. Humans who get stung by this fish usually die an agonizing death within days. However, it usually only attacks people when it feels threatened, or if you dare to go swimming wearing shiny objects.

The Glowfish can be eaten if the poison gland is removed properly. Their lumens gland is also used for a variety of other things. There were certain tribes and cities that once fished for the Glowfish and controlled the population, but war destroyed the city and the ancient custom died out, leaving Everly Lake fair game for the growing population of the deadly Glowfish. The city of Loradin at one point was especially afflicted with them because of its island location, and its gleaming beauty which was reflected in the water of Everly Lake by the sunlight.

They spawn and lay their glowing greenish eggs, by the hundreds, in their dark dens where they store all of their shiny water-soaked objects. Few eggs survive as they are not poisonous and are a favorite of other fish.

Native to and found only in Zanchier.

GLOWFISH

RIVERBRINE

Size = Ranges from a few inches to one foot in length.

Coloring = Mainly red and golden yellow but can vary depending on where they are caught.

Life Span = Varies.

Main Predators = Everything.

Riverbrine are shrimp-like crustaceans that thrive around the edges of Everly Lake near the shores of Reef Edge Village and the shoreline of the Xantifal Plains. However, they can be found throughout all waterways and lakes throughout Zanchier.

Unlike shrimp, they do not twitch to swim, but swim like a fish, flicking its long tail from side to side. They are caught and sold throughout Zanchier but are sold fresh daily in the mountain villages of Treeline Valley and Terra Valley. Some caught near the marshlands tend to have bioluminescent properties and this confused and frightened fishermen. Since then they are believed to be poisonous from this area, and so fishing near the marshlands has ceased. now no one goes near the marshlands. Ever.

Native to and found only in Zanchier.

HABITAT AREA WHERE MOSTLY FOUND.

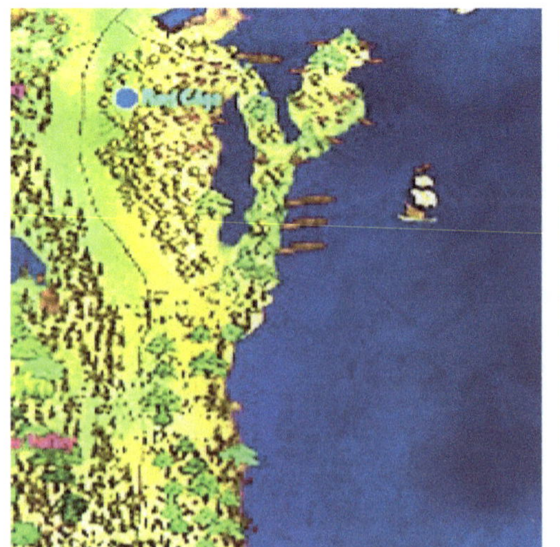
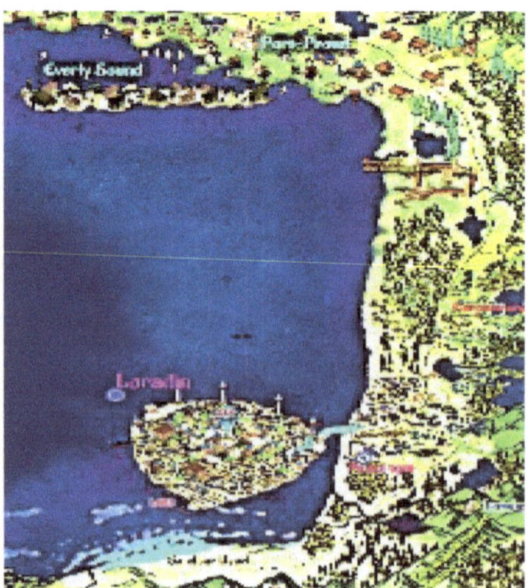

RIVERBRINE

ROCKHEAD

Size = Five foot in length at maturity.

Coloring = Mainly red and golden yellow fins with a greenish blue body.

Life Span = Varies.

Main Predators = Everything larger than it.

Rockhead fish are a thick-headed fish sought after for its flavorful, non-fishy, tasting meat. It is a thick bodied fish that is very meaty, and has few bones except for those near the head and the spine. It has no scales and is smooth to the touch.

They are often smoked and keep very well for long periods of time. Their larger fins and tails are often used for fish-stews mainly among the poorer people of Zanchier. They are a plentiful fish and are found throughout Everly Lake and in many other freshwater lakes across Zanchier.

Native to and found only in Zanchier.

HABITAT AREA WHERE MOSTLY FOUND.

ROCKHEAD

TREEHOUSE TREE

Type = Undetermined.

Size = Undetermined as no one can measure its length, with the exception that they are rather large in size.

Coloring = As most trees of Zanchier; brown trunk, leaves that turn shades of red, orange, yellow, purple, and teal in the fall and becomes bare in the winter.

Life Span = Undetermined as they have never been recorded.

OZ'S TREEHOUSE PLATFORMS

High atop the Xantifal Mountains is a certain type of rare tree.

These massively large trees grow extremely tall and wide.

No one knows what they are called as they only exist high up in the mountains where no one ever goes because of the deadly, man-eating, creatures that live up there. There are only a few dozen of them and all are above Catamount Gorge.

These unnamed trees grow even larger than the Giantrush trees that litter the valleys below Xantifal in the village of Treeline, Some villagers use the naturally hollowed basses of the Giantrush trees as homes or businesses.

The unnamed tree's branches, like most Zanchier trees, are so wide, thick, and long, that a person or creature can walk along them without fear of falling off. They intertwine with the rest of the large trees of Zanchier, making pathways above the ground. This can be safer for travel in some ways but deadlier in others if you happen to come across a Pagorinx along a branch.

Oz first discovered the tree house when he escaped the slave labor of the Rhe Mines. When he first found the tree there was sparse evidence that someone long ago had also used the hollowed-out tree as a home.

Native to and found only in the Xantifal Mountain ridgeline and below.

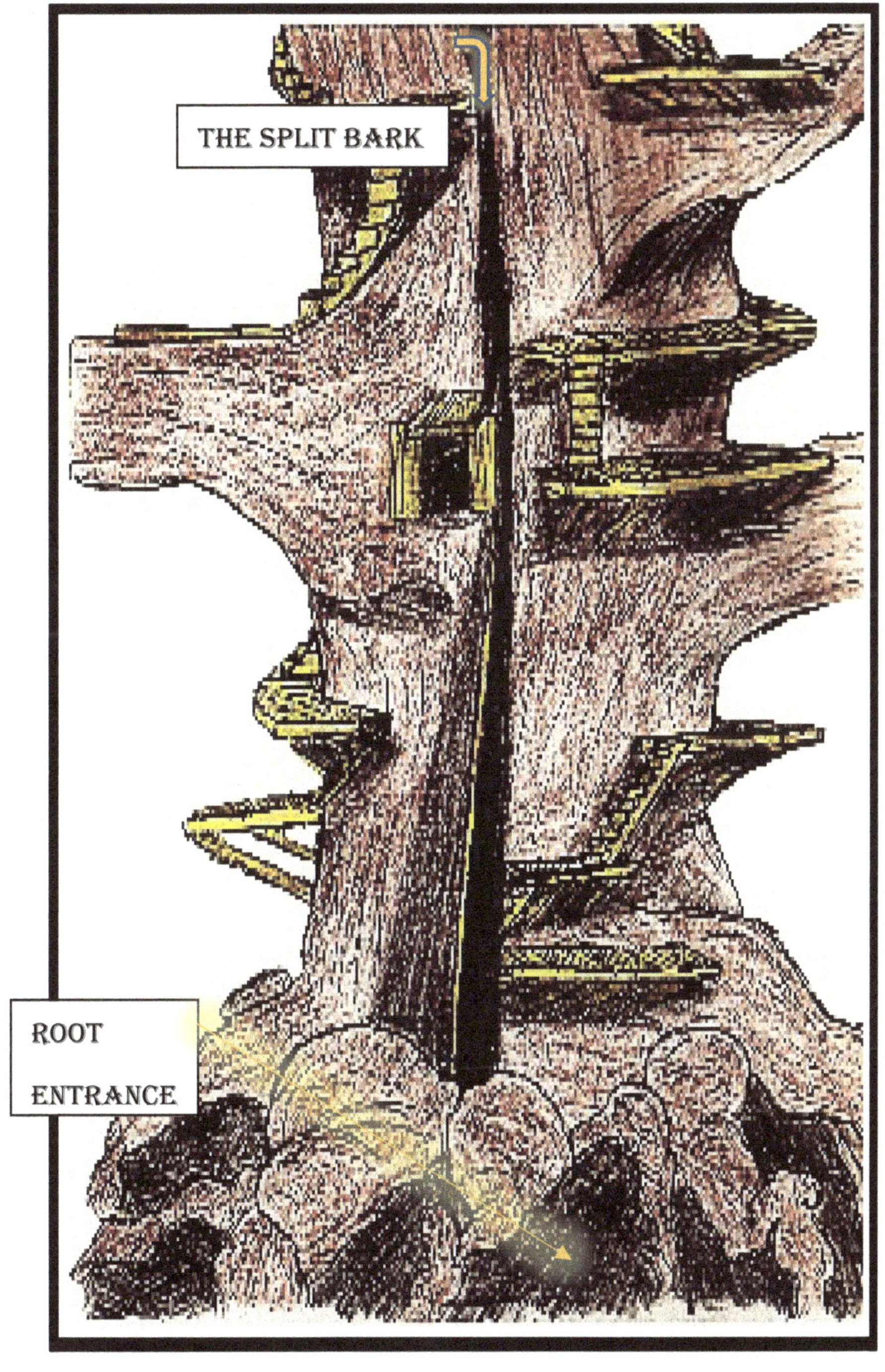
THE SPLIT BARK
ROOT
ENTRANCE

OZ'S TREEHOUSE INSIDE FACING FIREPLACE

This is the view you get when you walk through the wood and iron hewn door into the main living section of the treehouse. There is a stone fireplace that vents high up into the trees open center and out somewhere near the top through naturally made holes. The walls are mostly twisted together roots, and the floor is wood planks over a dirt and root base. There is a naturally made root stairway on each side of the tree's open center. The left stairway leads to a single open area which Oz made into his bedroom. The right-side stairway leads to another open area into the trees split section from where Oz added platforms that rise up and encircle the tree. When Bridget and Caroline appeared at his treehouse, he added another bedroom out of the open area at the top of the right-side stairway for the two of them.

OZ'S TREEHOUSE INSIDE FACING DOOR

This view is standing facing the doorway with the fireplace to the back. The root walls have a few natural knots that act as hangers for bags and such. Oz keeps his weapons close at hand beside the door. His furnishings are made from fallen trees and dried wood found along the Xantifal Mountain ridgeline.

TANMOYARO DRACONOMAI

The Mountain of the Dragons is home to the four weather dragons. This island exists on the fifth-dimension plane like the land of Zanchier. Which may explain why it was only accessible from Storm Valley. The plane where it resides is in the center of the Pacific Ocean near the Ring of Fire-which is a highly volatile, volcanic, area along the coastline which extends from the northern shores of America all the way around to the shores of Japan.

The weather dragons control the weather for all the realms, their demeanors lending to milder or stronger storms. The Wind Dragon lives in the floating mountains at the peak of the tallest spire. The Land Dragon roams the forest and jungles which surround the mountain's base. The Fire Dragon lives beneath the mountain base in a cavern, where the tunnels lead far below the earth's surface. The Water Dragon swims the oceans that surround the island. It often swims back and forth along the Ring of Fire, which would explain that regions volatile weather patterns.

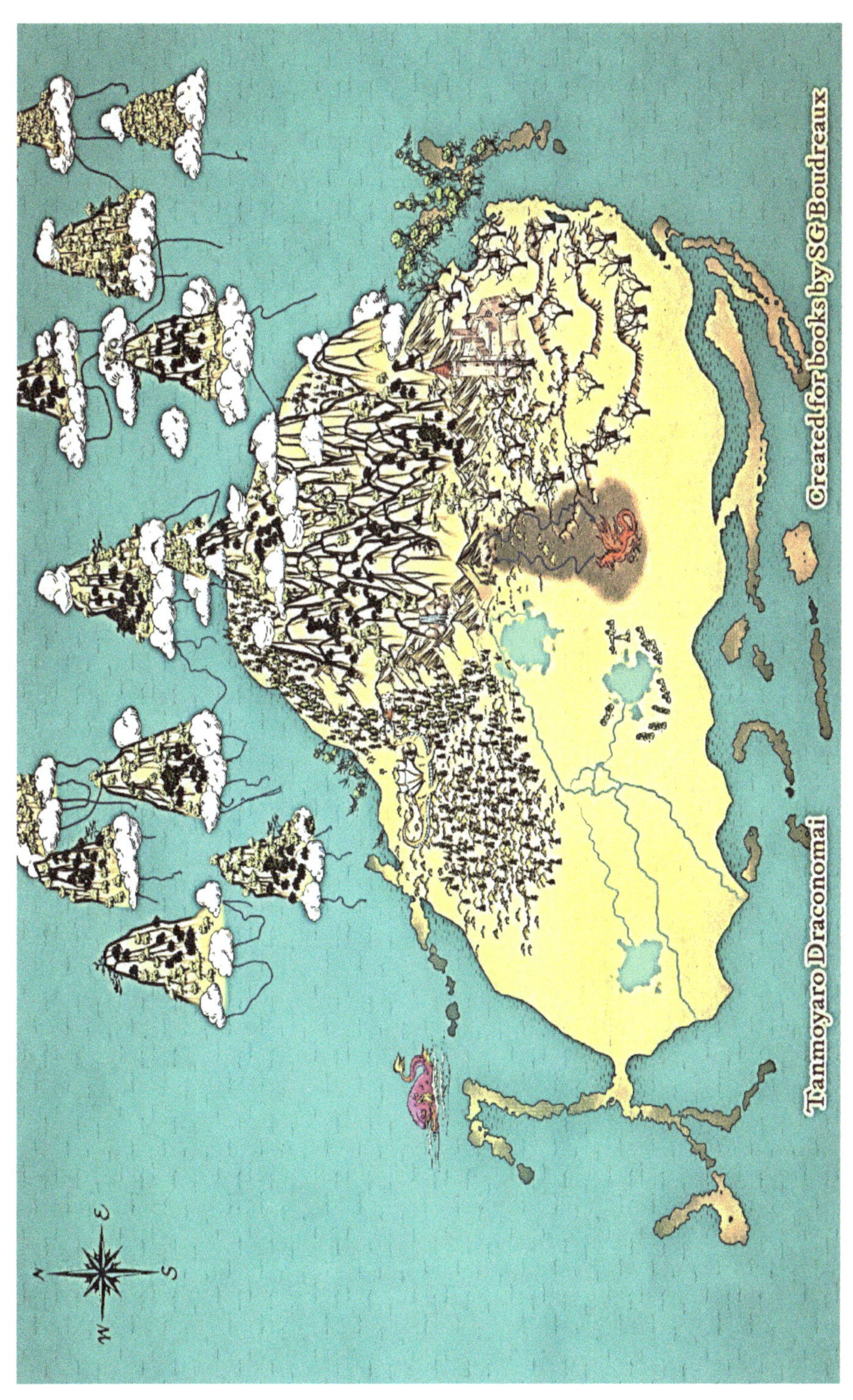
Created for books by S G Boudreaux
Tanmoyaro Draconomai
N
E
S
W

GARGANTHERA-LAND OF GIANTS

This country exists on the borderlands of Simon Lane's safehouse in the year 1580 B.C. The giant land is home to men and woman of all sizes, but the larger people tend to dominate the land. The animals, ships, carts, and buildings are just as large. It is a peninsula, as the backside borders mountains and forests, and the rest is surrounded by a large ocean with no other land to be seen from its shores.

Simon Lane frequented this city for supplies. Garganthera sits along Barrier's Edge just outside his safehouse in the year 1580 B.C,

Garganthea
Peregrination Series of Books
World of Giants
Designed by SG Boudreaux
Legend

READER'S ISLAND

This island is a respite for those chosen by God to serve as Peregrines, Dragoman, and Keepers. This forty-nine square mile island sits in the center of the Bermuda Triangle and is surrounded by the barrier. This barrier is the cause of the many disappearances of planes, boats, and other craft over the years.

The island boasts perfect weather, and that is based on the needs of each individual person. The northern side of the island is mostly forest and jagged rock. The eastern side is where the geyser and hidden cavern and temple sit just beneath the lighthouse. The prayer temple lays just northwest of the lighthouse and is surrounded by waterfalls, fountains, and an array of plant and animal life. The rambling Caribbean-style mansion is the permanent home and dwelling of the retired and injured Peregrines and Dragoman from the civil-war years ago. The mansion's thirty bedrooms, fourteen bathrooms, an archival library, a regular library, wardrobe room, computer room, large restaurant-sized kitchen, formal dining, and many other rooms houses many people. There are staff cottages behind the house just off the kitchen side. The top and bottom floor rooms boast French doors and each second-floor bedroom exits onto a wrap-around balcony. There is a horse stable and iron forge to the south. The feel of the island is so peaceful and calming that those who visit never want to leave.

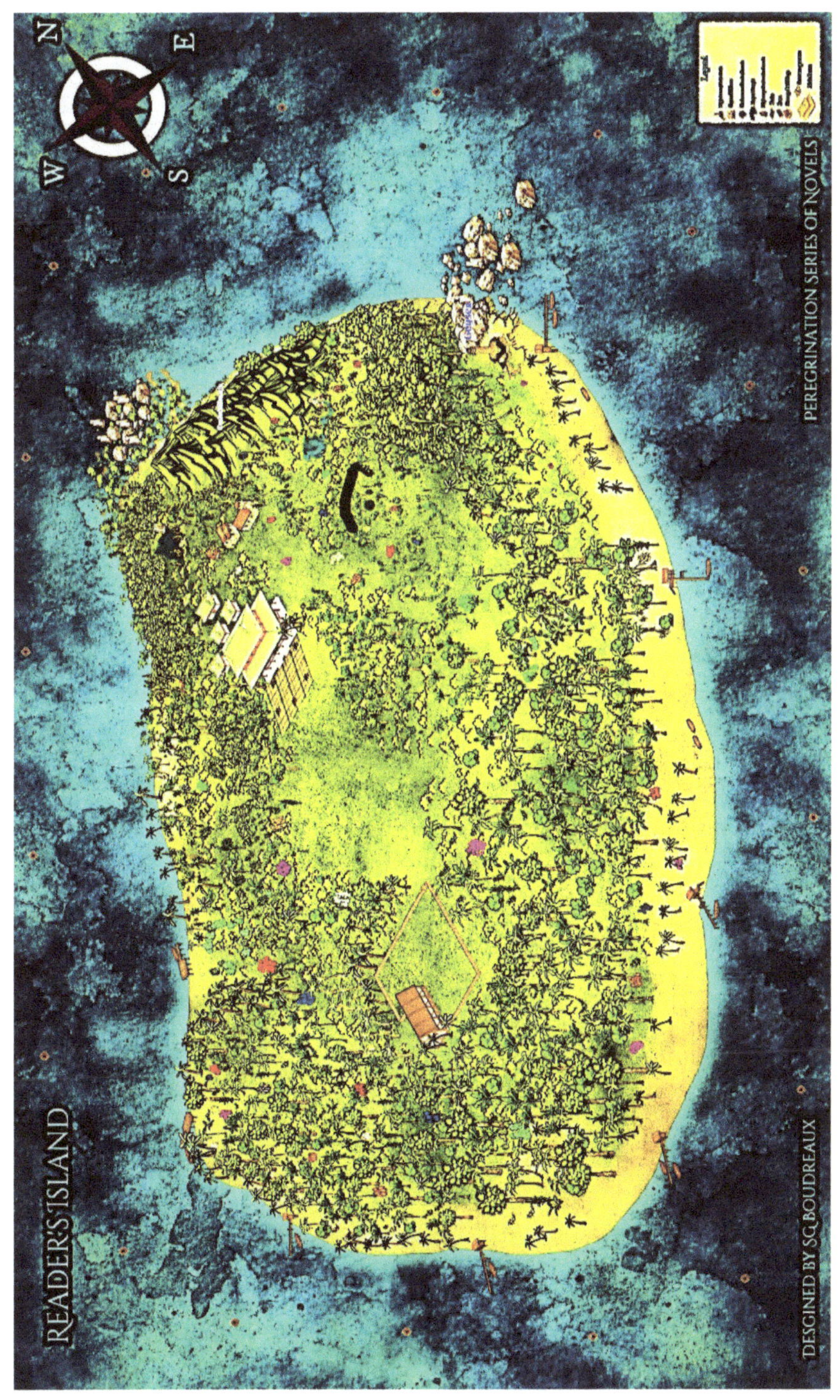
N
W
E
S
READER'S ISLAND
PEREGRINATION SERIES OF NOVELS
DESIGNED BY S.Q. BOUDREAUX

ZANCHIER

The world of Zanchier is a land-locked nation, or so those that live there believe. The cities, villages, and towns that exist around Everly Lake; the large central body of water; believe there to be no life outside of the Xantifal, Bakrashan, and Carpasian Mountain ranges. The white Mountains that border the northern territories and the southern marshlands are deadly, and no one dares to venture into or near the mountains. The Bleak mountains are crawling with deadly animals, and the Deadman's Desert and Dune Sea that borders the east and west sides of Zanchier are a wasteland that no one has ever heard reported as able to cross alive.

There is a constant civil unrest as Scaithers; a rogue band of evil men and women who care for no one; terrorize the entire nation. There is constant talks of impending war amongst the cities and Zanchieth rulers concerning the mining rights of the highly prized minerals of the Rhe Mines known as Rhenium and Ruthenium.

The academy graduates, by the age of sixteen, are placed into communities where their talents are used and they can benefit society. If children are not found to have a talent, they are placed into the harvest fields or the mines to serve out the remainder of their lives in lower income communities.

This Dystopian world of technological advancements, and some yet still archaic views and rules, is a contradiction in itself.

About The Author

SG Boudreaux is a stay-at-home mom who has home-schooled her children for over twenty years. Two have graduated, and her youngest is a nineteen-year-old, special-needs child. She and her husband of twenty-seven years live in the country, in a small rural area just outside of Lake Charles, Louisiana. She was born in West Virginia, lived in Florida for many years before moving to Louisiana with her mother and youngest sister. She married a local boy and has lived there ever since. She loves the culture, the people, the sense of community, and definitely the wonderful Cajun food. She is currently working on several new titles; one of which is the first book in a series of five books entitled The Stormwalker Series, which is fiction, fantasy, and time-travel. You can find out more about her and her books on her Facebook, Instagram, Twitter, or her website at www.sgboudreaux.com.

Her previous series of books include the Peregrination Series and the Zanchier Series, which are clean-reading, fiction, fantasy, and time-travel for middle grade and young adult readers but can be enjoyed by an age looking for fun, clean, reading.

Other Books

Peregrination Series

Zanchier Series

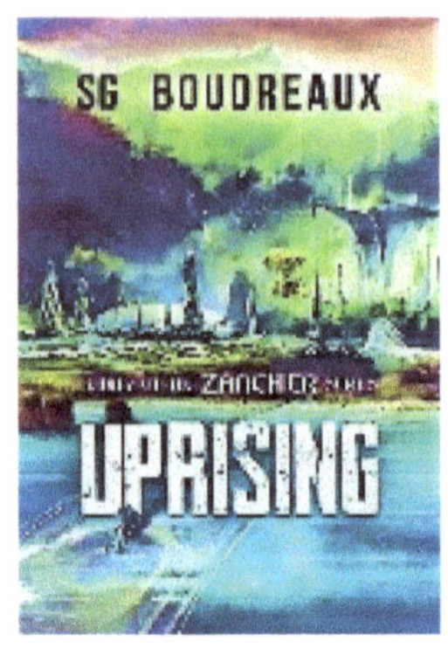

Romantic Comedy

Stormwalker Series

book 1 of 5 coming 2024

Non-Fiction Titles

www.ingramcontent.com/pod-product-compliance
Lightning Source LLC
Chambersburg PA
CBHW040231170726
48295CB00014B/877